THE Princess IN BLACK
and the GIANT PROBLEM

THE Princess IN BLACK
and the GIANT PROBLEM

Shannon Hale & Dean Hale

illustrated by
LeUyen Pham

CANDLEWICK PRESS

Text copyright © 2020 by Shannon and Dean Hale
Illustrations copyright © 2020 by LeUyen Pham

First edition 2020

Library of Congress Catalog Card Number pending
ISBN 978-1-5362-0222-9

20 21 22 23 24 25 LEO 10 9 8 7 6 5 4 3 2 1

Printed in Heshan, Guangdong, China

This book was typeset in LTC Kennerley Pro.
The illustrations were done in watercolor and ink.

Candlewick Press
99 Dover Street
Somerville, Massachusetts 02144

www.candlewick.com

For Sarah, Ann,
Hayley, Jamie,
and all our
Candlewick
heroes

Chapter 1

Snow lay all over Princess Magnolia's kingdom. It covered the pastures. It frosted the village rooftops. It piled beneath the castle windows.

Inside the castle, Frimplepants the unicorn curled up by the fire. He rested his chin on his hooves. Drowsy, he watched the flames dance.

Princess Magnolia was making a scrapbook. She glued photos and stuck stickers. She was just finishing a page about her birthday party. She sighed.

"I miss my princess friends," said Princess Magnolia.

Frimplepants nodded. He missed the princesses' pets, like his giraffe friend, Calypso Pete. And his tiger friend, Frizzfidget.

"I wish it was my birthday again," said Princess Magnolia, "so I could have a party. And invite all twelve of my princess friends."

Princess Magnolia had no party plans. However, the Princess in Black did have playdate plans. So Princess Magnolia put away her scrapbook.

"Time to change, Frimplepants," she said. And she winked.

It was cold outside. And Frimplepants had been just a whisker away from a nap. But he couldn't resist a snowy playdate.

Chapter 2

In the goat pasture, the goats had spent the morning hopping in the fluffy snow and burrowing in the puffy snow. So much fluffy-puffy snow. When their noses started to turn blue, Duff the Goat Boy led them into the goat shed.

The goat shed had blankets for cuddling. And straw for snuggling. Not to mention hot cocoa. Duff looked over his cuddled and snuggled herd. His work here was done.

So he put on a mask and a cape. And when he left the shed, he was no longer Duff the Goat Boy.

He was the Goat Avenger! And the Goat Avenger had a playdate.

The Princess in Black galloped into the goat pasture on her pony, Blacky. The Princess in Blankets trotted up on her unicorn, Corny.

"This is perfect snow for building," said the Princess in Black. "Let's make a snow monster and battle it for practice!"

The heroes rolled three big snow-balls and stacked them on top of each other. They added eyes and horns and claws. And then they waged battle.

The heroes knocked off the top part with mighty punches. They toppled the middle part with mighty kicks. Then they leaped onto the bottom part. Just for fun.

It was almost—*almost*—like a party.

The heroes built a second snow monster. And they were just about to battle it . . .

when a huge foot smashed the
snow monster flat.

"SQUASHY!" boomed a voice
from high above them.

Chapter 3

The three heroes looked up. A giant! Where had he come from? Not Monster Land. He was too big to fit through the hole.

"Hey, you squished our snow monster!" said the Princess in Black.

"SQUASHY!" roared the giant.

"Okay, then, you *squashed* our monster!" the Princess in Black yelled back.

The giant took a wobbly step. His foot came down on the Monster Land sign.

"SQUASHY," said the giant.

"Stop squashing things!" shouted the Princess in Blankets.

The giant took a step sideways. He smashed Duff the Goat Boy's second favorite reading chair.

"Behave, beast!" shouted the Goat Avenger.

The giant did not listen. He was too busy smashing a tree.

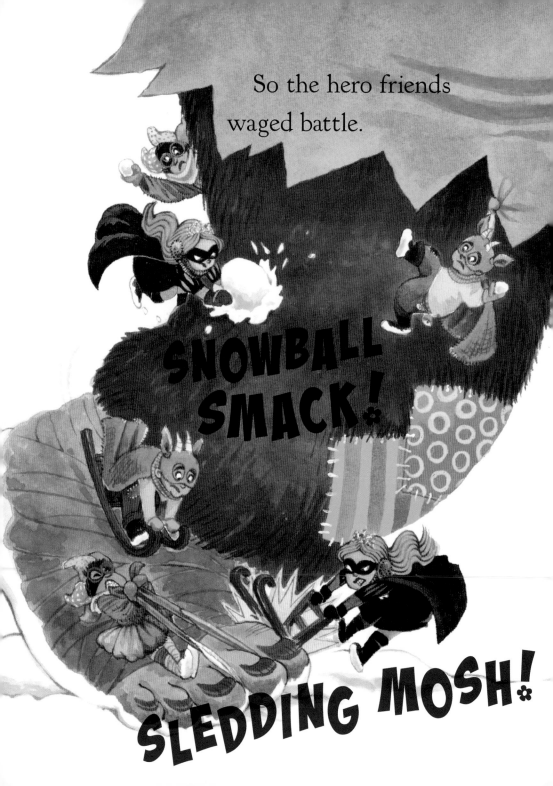

So the hero friends
waged battle.

SNOWBALL
SMACK!

SLEDDING MOSH!

The heroes waged battle. But the giant did not seem to realize a battle was being waged. He wandered away. A drop of drool fell from his mouth and plopped onto the snow. It froze into a lumpy icicle.

Chapter 4

Maybe the giant hasn't noticed us," said the Princess in Black. "Maybe we just need to explain."

The Princess in Black leaped up to the giant's knee. She lassoed the giant's ear and climbed the rope to his shoulder.

"Stop!" the Princess in Black shouted into the giant's ear. "You will hurt someone. You need to stop squashing—"

"SQUASHY!" said the giant. He hopped up and down. And the Princess in Black fell.

She fell right onto Blacky's back.
"Thank you, Blacky," she said.

"SQUASHY?" said the giant.

He started to stomp toward the
goat shed.

"Stop that giant!" said the Princess in Black.

The Goat Avenger and the Princess in Blankets were holding a long piece of twine. They stretched it in front of the giant's ankle. The giant took another step. But he did not trip on the twine. He did not come crashing down.

Instead, the giant just kept walking, and the two heroes, still holding on to the twine, were dragged along behind him.

"Ouch," said the Princess in Blankets.

"Ugh," said the Goat Avenger.

Being dragged behind a giant was no party.

"Three heroes isn't enough to stop a giant," said the Princess in Black. "We need help!"

"Help?" said the Princess in Blankets. "I've got an idea!"

But the Princess in Black didn't hear her idea. She was distracted by the giant. Who was still walking. And had almost reached the goat shed.

Chapter 5

F ly, Blacky, fly!" said the Princess in Black.

Blacky galloped to the goat shed. The Princess in Black leaped off Blacky's back and flung open the shed door. "You have to get out of here!" she said.

One goat sipped some cocoa.

"You're in danger!" said the Prin-cess in Black.

Another goat raised an eyebrow. They were always in danger, it seemed.

Then the giant yelled, "SQUASHY!"
The goats dropped their mugs of cocoa. And they ran.

Some say that goats do not run. But they are wrong. Goats do run. Especially if a giant is coming to squash them.

The giant picked up the empty goat shed. He stuck it in his mouth. He gnawed on it a bit.

"SQUASHY?" asked the giant.

Then he dropped the shed. The shed was now broken in two. And also gooey with drool.

"SQUASHY!" the giant roared. He stomped away.

"He seems upset," said the Princess in Blankets. "Maybe he ate too much cabbage. Too much cabbage makes me feel upset."

"I don't think cabbage is our problem right now," said the Princess in Black.

She pointed. The giant was headed toward the village.

"We have to stop him before he destroys the village," said the Goat Avenger.

"How?" asked the Princess in Black. "All three of us together aren't strong enough!"

"Maybe we need more than three of us," said the Princess in Blankets. She held up a pink stone and a flashlight.

"The Sparkle Signal!" said the Princess in Black. "Yes!"

The Princess in Blankets shone the flashlight through the stone. She aimed the beam of sparkly light into the sky.

Chapter 6

It was a cozy day in Princess Honeysuckle's kingdom. The snow was as high as the windows, and everyone was indoors.

Fur Suit the wolf sprawled beside the fire. The warmth was like a blanket. His eyelids felt heavy.

"Fur Suit, look!" said Princess Honeysuckle.

Fur Suit didn't want to look. He was just a tail hair away from a nap. But he rolled onto his feet. He trotted over to his princess, who was pointing out the window.

Outside, against the snow-filled clouds, shone a pink flower light.

"It's the Sparkle Signal!" she said. "Our friends need help!"

Fur Suit's heart pounded. His nap was forgotten.

The two shoved on their disguises.
And they became Cartwheel Queen
and her pet, Good Boy the dog.

Cartwheel Queen jumped onto his back. And Good Boy ran. He ran faster than any wolf in a dog collar had ever run.

"Let's take a shortcut through Princess Euphoria's kingdom!" said Cartwheel Queen.

Good Boy barked. Even though it was winter, the running made him feel as warm as if he were still lying beside the fire.

They were so busy running that they didn't notice Princess Euphoria and her pet giraffe sledding down a nearby hill.

"Look at that!" said Princess Euphoria, pointing up to the Sparkle Signal.

"Eeerp," said Calypso Pete, pointing a hoof at the masked hero riding a large dog.

"Hm," said Princess Euphoria. "Maybe the signal is a call for help. And heroes answer the call. Calypso Pete, I think it's time to try on our disguises."

Chapter 7

The Princess in Black, the Princess in Blankets, and the Goat Avenger stood in front of the giant. They waved their arms. They yelled, "Stop!" and "Go back!" and "Stay away from the village!"

The giant yelled, "SQUASHY?"

With enormous hands, the giant picked up all three heroes. And he stuck the Goat Avenger's legs in his mouth.

"You may not eat the Goat Avenger!" said the Princess in Black.

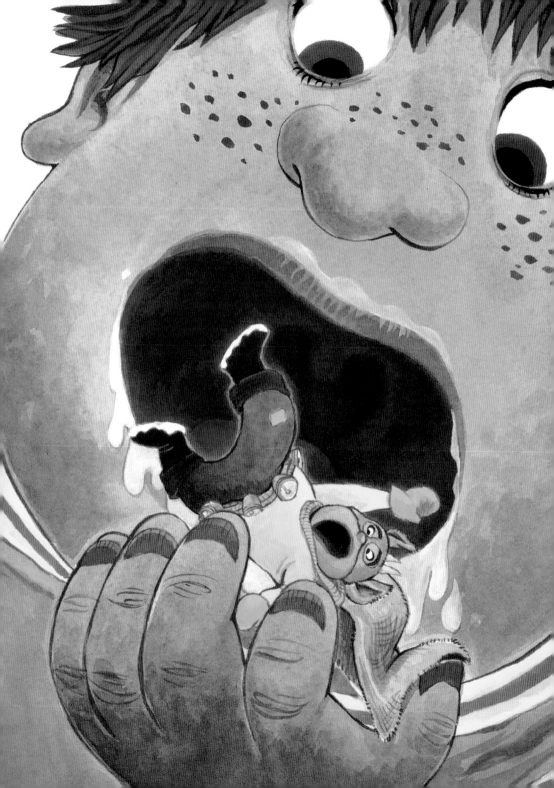

But the toothless giant didn't eat
the Goat Avenger. He just gnawed
on him with his gums. Then he said,
"SQUASHY. . ." and dropped them
all.

Landing headfirst in a pile of snow was *not* a party. The Goat Avenger's pants were wet with drool, but this was no time to change pants. The giant was getting closer to the village.

Just then, three new heroes arrived.

"Look!" said the Goat Avenger as he squeezed drool out of his pants. "It's Cartwheel Queen, Miss Fix-It, and Flower Girl!"

"They must have seen the Sparkle Signal!" said the Princess in Blankets.

"That's right!" said Cartwheel Queen. She did a cartwheel in the snow. "Could you use the help of three more heroes?"

"How about four?" said another new hero.

The six heroes gasped.

"I too saw your Sparkle Signal," said the new hero. "I'm Hopscotch, and this is my—"

"Giraffe?" said the Goat Avenger.

"Of course not," said Hopscotch. "Mr. Hiss is a snake!"

"Ah," said the Goat Avenger.

"We were only expecting three heroes," said the Princess in Black. "Four is better!"

"How about more?" said yet another new hero.

"Wow," said Miss Fix-It.

"Whoa," said Flower Girl.

"Great gobs of gum!" said the Princess in Blankets.

"Who are you all?" asked the Goat Avenger.

So the new heroes waged introductions.

SISTER SPARK AND HER NARWHAL, FISHY SPLASH!

RAIN BOW AND HER LION, ROAR BEAST!

"There are a lot of heroes now," the Goat Avenger started to say. But he was interrupted by more heroes.

LADY ROCK AND HER OCTOPUS, CUDDLEBUG!

VIOLET PILOT
AND HER PLANE, SILVER BELLE!

"Noseholes and elephants, so many heroes," the Princess in Blankets started to say. But she was interrupted. By more heroes.

SUN BLOCK AND HER SEA SNAIL, SLIM!

SUPER-MEOW AND HER CAT-FISH, PURR-MAID!

THE KICKER!

AND . . . COATRACK!

"Um . . ." said the Princess in Black, looking around. "Is that everybody?"

The new heroes and their pets all nodded.

"Oh, good!" said the Princess in Black. "Because we've got big trouble. And it's just about to squash the village."

Chapter 8

We put my little brother in a play-pen sometimes to keep him from eating the candles," Violet Pilot said. "Do we have a giant playpen to keep the giant from eating the village?"

"I have twine!" said the Princess in Blankets. She always had extra twine. And blankets.

"A piece of twine and two heroes wasn't enough to slow down the giant," said the Princess in Black. "But maybe a lot of heroes could use a lot of twine to make a playpen!"

"We flying heroes can distract the giant," said Flower Girl.

Flower Girl rode her pegasus, Horse-fly, around the giant's head. Violet Pilot and Silver Belle swooped in too. The giant stopped to look at them.

"SQUASHY?" he said.

Down below, each hero got a twine ball from the Princess in Blankets. They raced around the pasture, stretching twine between the trees. Soon the giant was sur-rounded by a twine playpen.

The giant started to walk toward the village again, but the twine fence was too high to step over. The giant pushed and pulled, but the twine fence was too strong to break.

The heroes were about to cheer! But then the giant began to cry.

"Wait, what?" the Goat Avenger said.

"S-S-SQUASHY . . ." the giant whimpered.

The heroes stood there. No one knew what to do when a giant cried.

Chapter 9

The giant continued to cry. Giant tears turned the snow to slush.

"What now?" whispered the Goat Avenger.

No one could hear him. The giant sobs were too loud.

"BOOM!" boomed a boom from far away in the mountains.

"Sounds like a storm," said Miss Fix-It.

Rain Bow looked at the sunny blue sky. "That's strange," she said.

"Yes, it is," said Sun Block.

"BOOM. BOOM. BOOM!" It almost sounded like shouting.

Violet Pilot circled on Silver Belle. She watched the mountains. "That's no storm," she said.

Flower Girl and Horsefly flew beside her. "That's a *somebody*."

And then they all heard words inside the BOOMS. "WHERE—IS—MY—BABY?"

With a booming step and a thunderous voice, an even more giant giant arrived. This giant was so huge, she crossed the goat pasture in one step. This giant was so enormous, her hair was full of clouds.

"POOR BABY," the big giant boomed. "DID YOU GET LOST?"

"SQUASHY," said the little giant. "SQUASHY LOST."

The big giant held out a huge fluffy squid. "HERE IS YOUR SQUASHY," she said.

"SQUASHY!" squealed the little giant. He grabbed the toy squid and hugged it.

"LET'S GO HOME," said the mama giant. She plucked the baby giant out of the twine playpen. In just a few giant steps, the two of them had disappeared back into the mountains.

Chapter 10

All the heroes just stood there. Mouths hanging open. Staring.

"So . . . it was a baby?" said the Goat Avenger. "This whole time? The big, huge, enormous giant really was just a *baby*?"

The heroes looked at one another. And then the heroes started to laugh.

They laughed so hard, they fell down in the snow. While they were down in the snow, they might as well make snow angels. So they did.

Making snow angels turned into building snow forts.

And naturally a snowball fight
came next. Not just any snowball
fight. The most gigantic snowball
fight any of them had ever seen.

"Now *this* is a party," said the
Princess in Black.

"We should have lots of parties,"
said Sun Block.

"Yes, every week!" said the Kicker.

"A weekly party, to keep in touch," said Hopscotch.

"And talk about how we can work together as heroes," said Sister Spark.

"And also just to party," said Lady Rock.

"That's exactly what I was thinking," said the Princess in Black. And she rolled another snowball.